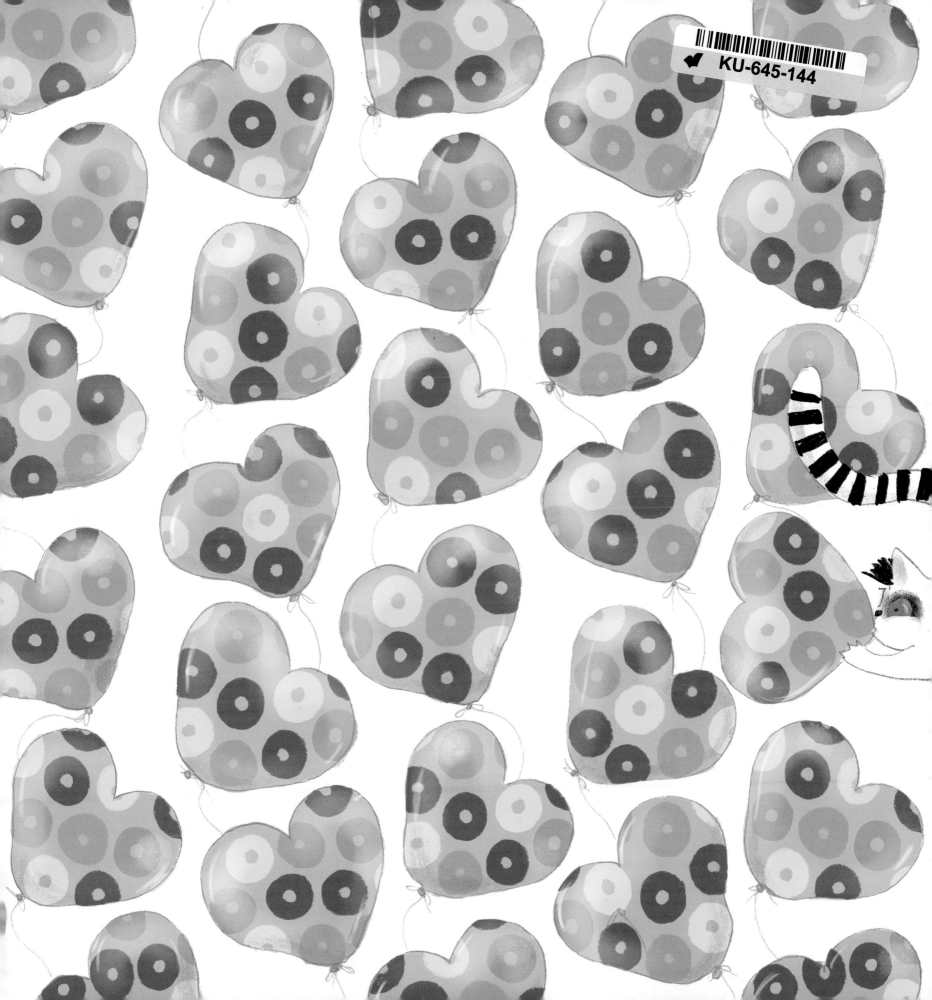

For Richard and Gabrielė

First published in Great Britain in 2019 by Hodder and Stoughton

Copyright © Steve Antony 2019

Hodder Children's Books
An imprint of Hachette Children's Group
Part of Hodder and Stoughton
Carmelite House
50 Victoria Embankment
London, EC4Y 0DZ

ISBN 978 1 44495 678 8

1 3 5 7 9 10 8 6 4 2

Printed in China

An Hachette UK Company
www.hachette.co.uk

Hodder
Children's
Books

MIX
Paper from
responsible sources
FSC® C104740

We Love You, Mr Panda

Steve Antony

FREE
HUGS

I need a hug.

OK, Skunk. Let's have a hug.

I love you, too.

I was talking to Croc.
I love you, Croc.

May I please have a hug?

OK, Elephant. Let's have a hug.

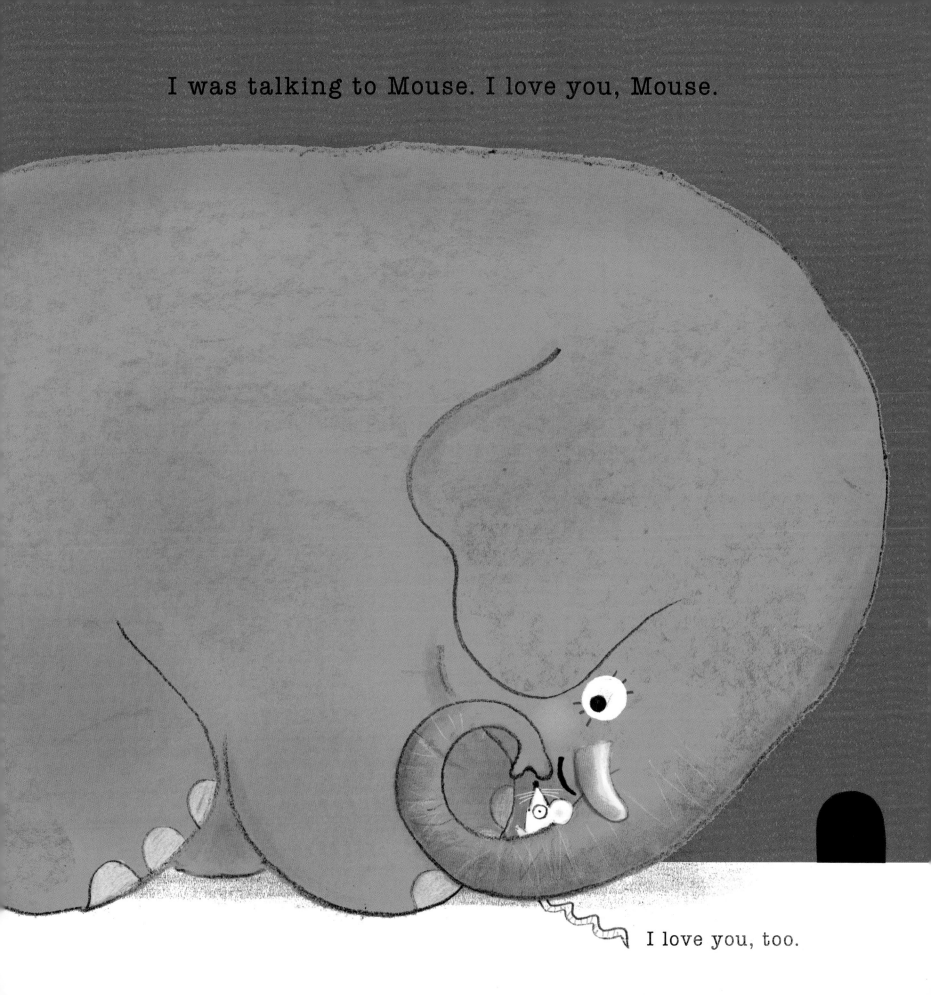

Would you like a hug, Sloth?

No thanks, Mr Panda.
I can hug myself.

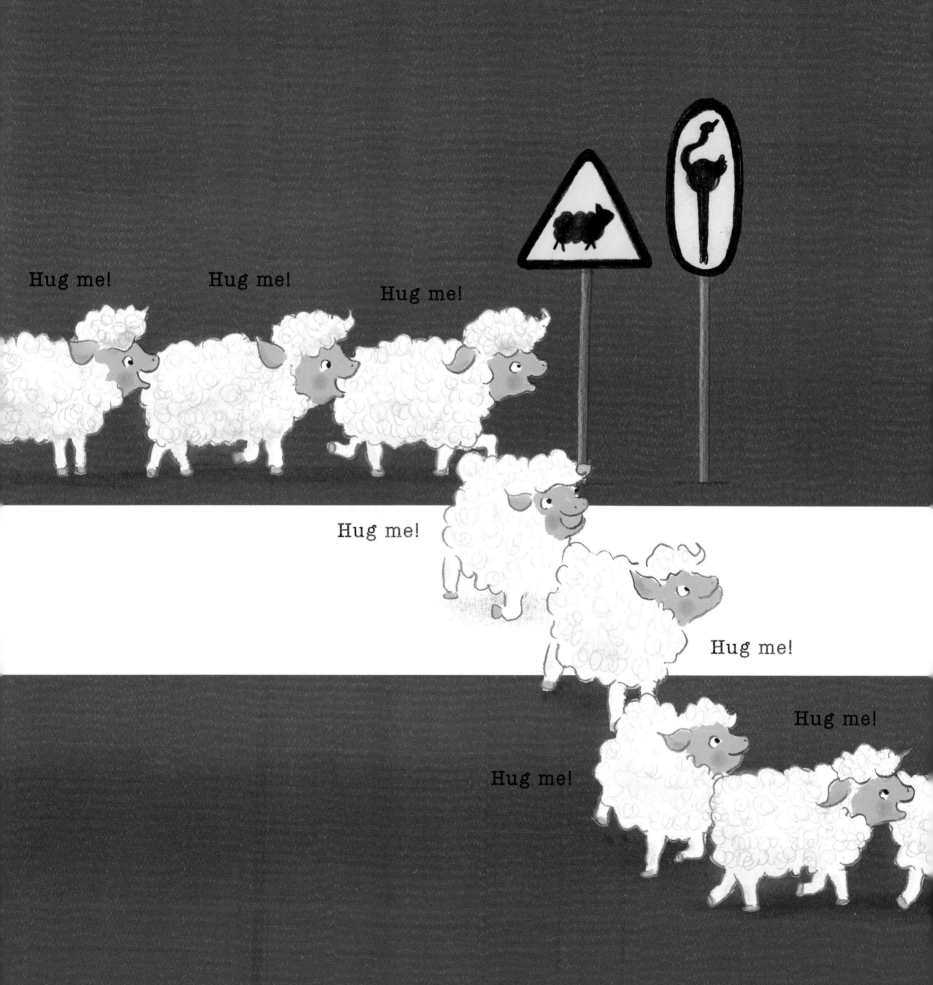

OK, sheep. Let's have a hug.

FREE HUGS

Hug me!   Hug me!   Hug me!   Hug me!   Hug me!   Hug

We were talking to Ostrich.
We love you, Ostrich.

I love you all, too.

I guess nobody

wants my hugs . . .

Don't go, Mr Panda.

Would YOU like a hug?

No, I would not like a hug . . .

. . . I would LOVE a hug. Thank you.

And so would we!

We love you, Mr Panda!

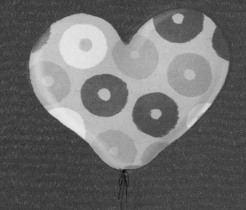

I love you, too.

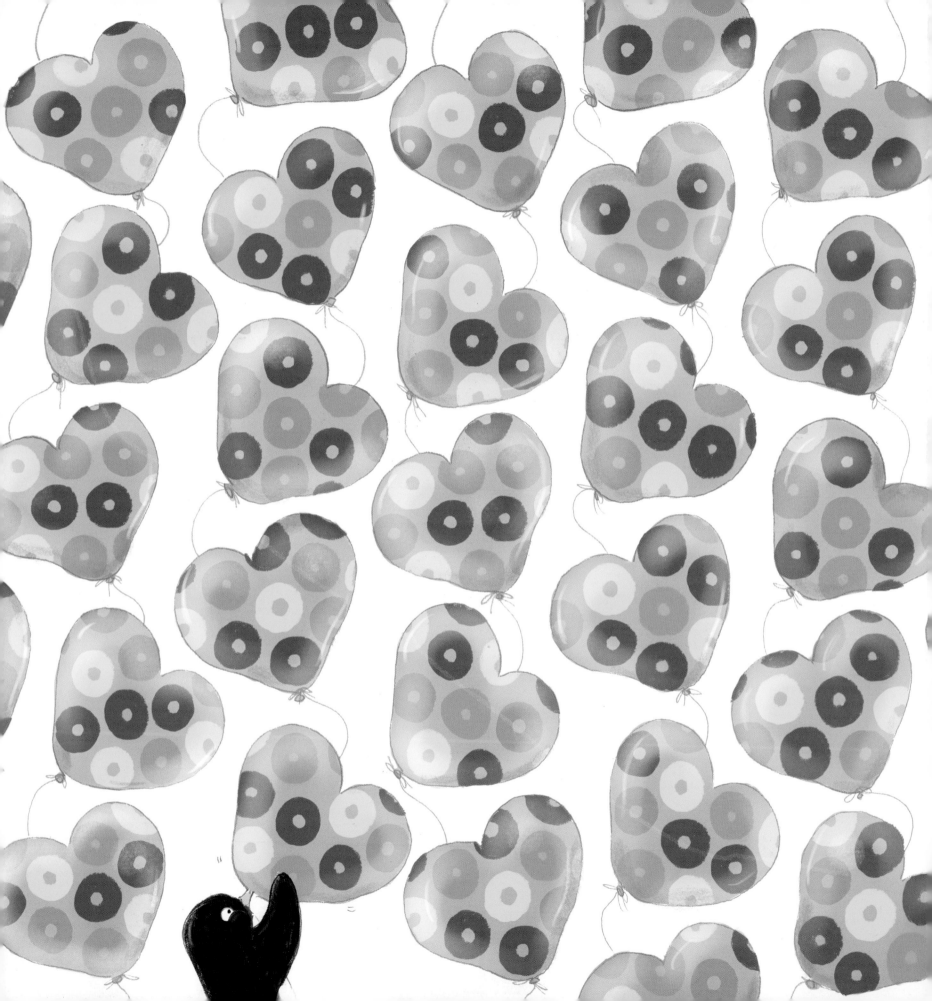